Horace and Morris
Say Cheese
(which makes Dolores sneeze!)

Super Tasty

To Zoey—for her love of cheese, and my love of her
—J. H.

For my uncle Ned McNally and my uncle Gene Walrod,
both of whom fought their own courageous battles
—A. W.

ATHENEUM BOOKS FOR YOUNG READERS
An imprint of Simon & Schuster Children's Publishing Division
1230 Avenue of the Americas, New York, New York 10020
Text copyright © 2009 by James Howe
Illustrations copyright © 2009 by Amy Walrod
All rights reserved, including the right of reproduction in whole or in part in any form.
ATHENEUM BOOKS FOR YOUNG READERS is a registered trademark of Simon & Schuster, Inc.
For information about special discounts for bulk purchases, please contact Simon & Schuster
Special Sales at 1-866-506-1949 or business@simonandschuster.com.
The Simon & Schuster Speakers Bureau can bring authors to your live event. For more information or to book an event,
contact the Simon & Schuster Speakers Bureau at 1-866-248-3049 or visit our website at www.simonspeakers.com.
Also available in an Atheneum Books for Young Readers hardcover edition.
The text for this book is set in Gararond.
The illustrations for this book are rendered in acrylic on paper.
Manufactured in China
0711 SCP
First Atheneum Books for Young Readers paperback edition October 2010
4 6 8 10 9 7 5 3
The Library of Congress has cataloged the hardcover edition as follows:
Howe, James, 1946–
Horace and Morris say cheese (which makes Dolores sneeze!) / by James Howe ; illustrated by Amy Walrod.—1st ed.
p. cm.
Summary: The timing could not be worse for Dolores the mouse when she develops a food allergy to
yummy cheese right before the Everything Cheese Festival.
ISBN 978-0-689-83940-5 (hc)
[1. Cheese—Fiction. 2. Allergy—Fiction. 3. Mice—Fiction.] I. Walrod, Amy, ill. II. Title.
PZ7.H83727Hh 2009
[E]—dc22
2003019608
ISBN 978-0-689-87177-1 (pbk)

Horace and Morris Say Cheese
(which makes Dolores sneeze!)

by JAMES HOWE

illustrated by AMY WALROD

ATHENEUM BOOKS FOR YOUNG READERS
NEW YORK   LONDON   TORONTO   SYDNEY

Horace and Morris but mostly Dolores loved to eat cheese.

They ate string cheese and Swiss cheese on Sundays.

They ate Muenster with mustard on Mondays.

They ate Roquefort and Beaufort and Blarney and blue. Romano, parmigiano, and Waterloo, too. They ate cheddar with their chowder and feta with their fritters. There was no cheese they would not eat.

Look, Dolores is covered with spots!
They're kind of pretty.
They itch!
OUR SCRAP-BOOK OF cheese
MAGIC GLUE

Doctor Ricotta looked at Dolores. She looked at her notes.
She looked back at Dolores. She looked back at her notes.
She wiggled her nose.

"What is it?" Dolores's mother asked.
"Dolores is allergic to cheese," said Doctor Ricotta.
"That is why she is sneezing and breaking out
 in itchy spots."

Dolores could not imagine life without cheese.
It was her **favorite** thing to eat!

Her mother tried to help. She gave her pumpkin seed
cookies on Mondays. She gave her poppy seed cookies on
Tuesdays. And every day she gave her a peanut butter
sandwich cut into a different shape.

Dolores was beginning to imagine life without cheese. But then . . .

But Dolores didn't want to go visit her aunt Wanda or hide under her bed. She wanted to go to the Everything Cheese Festival and eat all the cheese she could eat.

From that moment on, all Dolores could think about was cheese, **cheese**, cheese.

"I'm never eating cheese again," Dolores moaned.

Day after day, Dolores ate her peanut butter sandwiches and tried not to think about the Everything Cheese Festival, which was getting closer and closer.

"I'm sick of peanut butter sandwiches," Dolores said at last. "Who cares what shape they are? They always taste the same."

Suddenly she had an idea. She opened her sandwich, crumbled a pumpkin seed cookie inside, and asked each of her friends to give her something to add.

Her new sandwich was delicious!

This gave her an even better idea. . . . .

Dolores discovered there was more to life than cheese. . . .